Silent Night
✦ A MOUSE TALE ✦

BETSY HERNANDEZ AND DONNY MONK
ILLUSTRATED BY JOE BODDY

SPARROW

SPARROW PRESS
Nashville, Tennessee

Library of Congress Cataloging-in-Publication Data

Hernandez, Betsy.
    Silent night : a mouse tale / by Betsy Hernandez and Donny Monk :
illustrated by Joe Boddy.
         p.   cm.
    Summary: Relates the important part Strauss Mouse and his family
played in the creation of one of the world's most beloved Christmas
carols, "Silent Night."
    ISBN 0-917143-10-8 : $12.95
    [1. Mice—Fiction.   2. Christmas—Fiction.]   I. Monk, Donny,
1949-   II. Boddy, Joe, ill.   III. Title.
PZ7.H43173S1   1992
[E]—dc20

                                          92-28852
                                            CIP
                                            AC

Published in Nashville, Tennessee, by Sparrow Press,
and distributed in Canada by Christian Marketing Canada, Ltd.

Printed in the United States of America
96 95 94 93 92   5 4 3 2 1

Design by Jim Vienneau

For my faithful teammate, Frank, and our two kids,
Evan and Tiffany Hart—B.H.

To my father, J. Roark Monk, and my wife, Kathy,
two people who believe in me and my dreams.
For Tyler and Timothy, who helped me write the book.—D.M.

"Silent Night" is one of the world's most-loved Christmas carols. But it might never have been written without the help of a family of church mice.

It all started in Oberndorf, Austria, when the choral music prepared for the Christmas Eve service in 1818 had to be cancelled, because something—or someone—had destroyed the bellows of the church's pipe organ. This made some people very upset. But two men, Franz Gruber and Joseph Mohr, found a way to preserve the Christmas joy—and they learned that God, who loves all His creatures, will sometimes work in mysterious ways. And in the end, one little mouse in particular found out that... Well, why don't we start at the beginning and you'll see for yourself.

Si-lent night, ho-ly night, All is calm all is bright Round yon vir-gin mother and child Ho-ly In-fant so tender and mild, Sleep in heav-en-ly peace, Sleep in heav-en-ly peace

It was the coldest winter anyone could remember in the little town of Oberndorf. The drifting snow made the countryside look like windswept mounds of whipped cream, dotted with miniature gingerbread houses. Smoke circled heavenward from tiny red chimneys. A few brave souls scurried among the houses and shops with their collars turned up against the bitter wind. Some glanced at the heavy clouds overhead with a shudder, thankful for the promise that Christmas was near.

In the center of town, light flickered through the stained-glass windows of St. Nicholas Church. The wind whistled around its lofty spire.

Inside, a small group huddled beneath the towering pipes of the old organ, rubbing their hands for warmth while rehearsing the special music to be presented on Christmas Eve. They were unaware of a small, furry visitor watching quietly from his hiding place under a pew. He carefully peeked out with a twitching nose, waiting for just the right moment.

Franz Gruber, the organist and leader of this tiny choir, was patiently coaching Frau Hagglemeir who couldn't seem to remember when to come in for her solo. She had sung in every Christmas program at the church for forty years. Age had replaced the sparkle in her voice with an annoying warble. This caused her chin (and the heads of her listeners) to bob up and down sympathetically with every beat. Several choir members were getting restless and rolled their eyes as Franz was about to cue Frau Hagglemeir one more time. He gave an obvious nod in her direction at just the right time when...

Eeeeeeek!" she shrieked a note higher than any ever written for the human voice. "*A mouse!*" Frau Hagglemeir shot straight up into the air and perched on the back of the highest pew.

"Don't worry," Franz tried to console her. "They won't hurt you."

"You m-m-mean there are *more* of them?" trembled Frau Hagglemeir.

"Well...yes," he said. "They keep me company late at night...when I'm working."

Frau Hagglemeir pointed a stubby finger at Franz and shook it in his face. "I demand that you get rid of all those horrid little creatures. Tomorrow is Christmas Eve, and I will not sing in a church full of mice!"

It took two of the strongest men in the choir to help the distressed woman climb down from her perch. She snatched up her shawl, tucked the loosened strands back into her hair bun and, with a huff, marched out the door.

When Franz had ushered the last choir member out, he closed the door and breathed a deep sigh. "Well, at least she shrieked where her solo was supposed to come in." He leaned against the door and looked up. "Lord," he prayed, "I just don't have the heart to hurt my little mouse friends. They've always looked to me for bits of food and protection. How could I destroy them now?"

*F*rom a small hole in the wall behind the organ, came faint, squeaky laughter.

"Friedle! Did you see that old lady jump?!"

"Oh, Strauss! I bet she hasn't moved that fast in years!"

Suddenly, their laughter was cut short. Mama Mouse, who happened to see her son's mischief, was now making her way quickly towards the two younger mice. "Strauss!" she said sternly, "you should be ashamed of yourself! Scaring that poor old lady!"

"But Mama," Strauss whined. "The dishes start walking off the shelf every time she hits that awful note. My finely-tuned, musical mouse ears just couldn't take it any more!"

Mama shook her head. "You were too busy laughing to hear what she said. She wants Franz to get rid of us all now!"

"Oh, Mama! Not Franz," assured Friedle.

"He wouldn't hurt a flea!" said Strauss, scratching his ear. "He's a kind man. A musician—like I'm going to be someday. Anyway, what's a church without church mice?"

Mama did not laugh. Papa Mouse had come in, and they looked at each other with eyes full of concern.

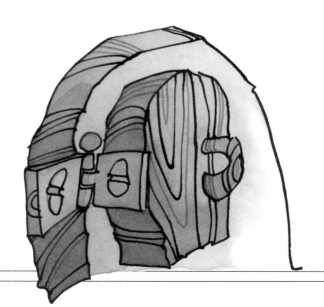

ranz was gathering his music and his thoughts when a voice startled him from the back of the church.

"Working late again?"

The voice belonged to Joseph Mohr, the young pastor who had become a good friend to Franz.

"Joseph! You scared me," gasped Franz, reaching for the music he had just spilled across the floor.

"I'm sorry," chuckled Joseph. "Here, let me help you."

As they picked up the pieces of scattered music, Franz told Joseph all about Frau Hagglemeir, the mouse and the ruined choir rehearsal. He sighed, "Maybe we'll have a blizzard on Christmas Eve and nobody will be able to come."

"That bad, is it?" said Joseph, looking at his friend. "It must be hard when your heart is dreaming of symphonies and your ears are hearing the strained efforts of a small village choir." He handed Franz a piece of music he had retrieved from under the organ pedals. "Looking for this?"

"*Danke schön*... Oh my! Frau Hagglemeir's solo. What would we have done without this?"

"Oh my, yes!" said Joseph with a gleam in his eye. "We do have a tradition to uphold, you know." The two men laughed together. Joseph always knew how to make Franz feel better.

They stepped outside the church.

"Franz?" said Joseph kindly. "Have you ever thought that God might not be so impressed with all our efforts to make grand and glorious music? He may prefer a simple song from a sincere heart. That's what I see in you. Heaven knows our little choir is not the best in the world, but it's the best we've got around here. Sometimes, I even see a little of that sincere heart of yours coming out in them."

"I hope you're right," sighed Franz.

Joseph closed the door as they turned to make their way home through the glistening snow.

As soon as the church door clicked shut, a rustling could be heard from inside the far wall.

"Are they gone?" said a squeaky whisper.

"Sh-h-h-h!" said another, cautiously. "Let me see for sure."

A tiny black nose poked through the mouse hole beside the organ and then quickly disappeared. "They're gone!" said the mouse voice more boldly. "Come on everybody! Christmas is two days away. Tomorrow will be Christmas Eve. So that makes tonight Christmas Eve *Eve*! Time to decorate for tomorrow's celebration."

Suddenly, mice came from everywhere, scurrying around and chattering all at once.

"I've got a shiny button!" squeaked Tiny Tot mouse.

"And I've found some bright red berries," offered Herr Whiskers.

"Does anyone have some bread crumbs?" asked Auntie Wiggletail. "I've been saving this raisin to make a bread pudding! Yum! Yum!"

What a happy time it was for the mice! Grandpapa Twitch Earheimer gathered the smallest mice around him to tell the story of his great, great, great grandcestors who were in the very stable where the baby Jesus was born. All the other mice were singing merrily as they worked.

*D*uring all the hustle and bustle, Strauss and Friedle climbed up the pipes of the great organ. They sat on the edge of the tallest pipe to watch the activities below.

"Friedle, someday I'm going to be a great composer," said Strauss wishfully. "Then *everyone* will hear my songs."

"And I want to be a great singer," replied Friedle dreamily. "With my voice, I'll soar like a bird to the very tip-top of the high notes."

"Just like Frau Hagglemeir?" Strauss teased. Then he stood up, with his nose pointed in the air, and warbled. His chin bobbed up and down. And then, just as he hit the highest note...

"*Ah-h-h-h-h-eeeeeee-yow!*" Strauss lost his balance and fell backwards into the tallest organ pipe!

Down.

Down.

Down he went and landed *kerplunk* in the bottom of the huge organ!

"Strauss! Where are you?" yelled Friedle. "Are you all right? I'll go get help!"

Strauss Mouse lifted his head, shook himself and moaned painfully. "*Oooh.* Wh-where am I?" It didn't feel as if anything was broken, so he got up slowly. He could barely see the light at the top of the pipe he had fallen into. "I've got to find another way out of here. It's too far to climb back up."

For a long time, Strauss groped through the darkness inside the organ, winding through the maze of pipes and levers. There seemed to be no way out and he was beginning to feel very weak. Frightened and discouraged, he put his head down and started to cry. "I'm really lost! What if I'm stuck in here forever?"

Strauss sat there in the dark silence for a minute—or was it an hour? Wait! Was his mind playing tricks on him or could that really be Friedle and some of the other mice calling to him? He felt around and realized that he was inside the leather accordion-like bellows at the back of the organ. He called out as loudly as he could, "Here I am! Can you hear me?"

"Hold on, Strauss!" came Friedle's reply.

Outside the organ, Papa Mouse looked over the situation and decided, "We'll have to chew through the bellows to get him out!"

The mice began working on the thick leather with their sharp teeth.

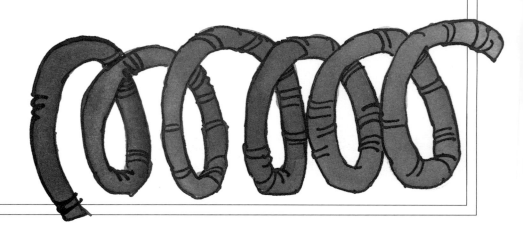

*F*inally, Strauss Mouse was free.

Mama Mouse hugged her son tightly. "Honestly, Strauss!" she said, relieved. "The trouble you get into! Poor Grandpapa Twitch Earheimer has probably ruined his new false teeth chewing through those bellows."

"I'm sorry, Mama!" said Strauss. He began to sob. "Look at the organ! It's ruined, too!" All the mice turned to look at the tattered shambles that had once been the heart and lungs of the old, majestic instrument.

"Poor, poor Franz," sighed Friedle sadly. "What will he do now?"

Christmas Eve dawned bright and beautiful, with the sun dancing playfully on the crystal white snow. But nothing could lighten the gloom in Strauss Mouse's heart. He knew that soon the choir members would be coming for practice and the broken organ would be discovered. Franz had been so kind to protect the lives of the Mouse family—and this is what had come of it. How could he ever find it in his heart to forgive them? Strauss was certain that the Mouse family would now be driven out into the cold—*or worse*. He sighed tearfully, "And it's all my fault."

Joseph was shovelling coal into the potbellied stove, while Franz was arranging his music on the organ.

"Joseph," Franz said, "would you mind pumping the bellows while I practice this difficult part of the music one more time?"

"Not at all," replied Joseph. The choir members were beginning to arrive. He nodded in welcome as he made his way through the door at the back of the massive instrument. Inside the small room, he slipped his feet into the stirrups on top of the bellows, held on to the brass handles and began to pump with his feet.

Franz pressed keys... Not a sound. "Joseph, are you pumping?"

"*Pssst!* Franz!" Joseph stuck his head out through the door and motioned for Franz to come. He was trying not to draw the attention of the assembling choir, but he looked worried.

Strauss Mouse watched sadly from his perch above the door, as Joseph showed Franz the ruined bellows. "With a hole that big, the organ will never play," said Joseph. "And we can't patch it."

*J*ust then Frau Hagglemeir paraded through the door. "Why are we late getting started? Is there a problem here?" she asked.

Joseph and Franz could not hide the shredded bellows. It was obviously the work of little mouse teeth.

"Oh my!" Frau Hagglemeir gasped as she fell back with a thud against the door frame. The sudden jolt shook Strauss Mouse, who lost his footing and toppled—wouldn't you know it!—right onto the tightly wound bun on Frau Hagglemeir's head!

She was too upset to notice her new hairpiece and so she proceeded, "Herr Gruber! Because you did not follow my instructions to rid this church of those filthy, horrid mice, our precious organ is ruined, along with our Christmas Eve program *and* my solo. Why...Why...You've ruined Christmas for everyone!"

Frau Hagglemeir went on and on wagging her head back and forth with each new outrage, and nodding up and down with every wave of her short, stubby finger. Strauss was having a terrible time trying to hang onto the wild, bucking hair bun.

"You can be sure," she threatened, "that the day after Christmas I will be here early in the morning with my two cats, Fritz and Adolph! They will make quick work of those beasty little mice. You won't be able to find heads or tails, feet or fur when *my* cats are through!"

By now all the choir members were aware of the disturbance. But no one, especially Joseph and Franz, had the courage to tell Frau Hagglemeir about the poor frightened mouse clinging to her hair bun.

ithout warning, Frau Hagglemeir twirled around to make her exit. The sudden spin left Strauss hanging on for dear life—with his tail dangling right between her eyes!

The ruffled old lady crossed her eyes and finally saw what everyone else had been staring at. It was too much! "Oo-o-o-o-h..." She sank to the floor in a faint.

What happened next was nothing less than total confusion...

Exhausted, Strauss hoped no one had seen him scramble into Franz's guitar. He decided to stay put until he could slip away unnoticed.

When the church was empty and still again, Joseph and Franz sat down to breathe in the peaceful silence.

"I guess I should have gotten rid of those mice," Franz said slowly. "But somehow I think they trust me." He shook his head. "And now, with no organ, maybe Christmas *is* ruined."

Joseph looked out the window thoughtfully. "Franz," he said after a moment. "Last night I saw something so wonderful I don't think anything could spoil *this* Christmas for me. Do you know the Dunderhof family?"

"I believe so. Isn't he the woodcutter whose wife just had a baby?"

"Yes. I went to see them and bless the child. Their home was so simple, so poor, offering little more shelter than a stable. It was like walking into a living Nativity scene. Looking into that baby's beautiful, innocent face reminded me of the true reason for the music and celebration."

"What do you mean?" questioned Franz.

"Christmas. The day the Son of God became a baby—a helpless baby in a manger. Think of it. *He became one of us!*"

"Yes," said Franz, thinking. "That *is* what Christmas is really about."

Joseph pulled a folded piece of paper from his coat pocket and handed it to Franz. "On the way home from the Dunderhof's, I wrote down some of my thoughts in a poem. I wonder if you can do anything with it."

*F*ranz read the words quietly.

"Silent Night, Holy Night
All is calm, all is bright..."

Franz did not hide the tears coming to his eyes as he finished reading the poem. "Beautiful!" he whispered.

"You may not have an organ, Franz," said Joseph, "but your guitar is over there in the corner. Let's see if you can find a melody to fit the words."

Joseph crossed the room, picked up the instrument and handed it to Franz.

Like a miracle, the song came. Its simple melody and chords fit the words perfectly. As the two men sang it together for the first time, they did not know they already had an audience, a trembling little mouse, who was still hiding inside the guitar.

*T*hat night, the faithful gathered from all over the countryside. Some had travelled far, from hidden valleys wedged between the snow-covered Austrian Alps. The church was a warm refuge from the cold wind. Christmas candles filled the room with a welcoming glow.

In the end, no one really missed the organ music—not even Frau Hagglemeir. The silence seemed to speak to each heart. Joseph read the Christmas story with new feeling and shared his experience at the woodcutter's home. Franz came forward to join the young pastor and together, with only a guitar, they sang the song from heaven.

When the Christmas Eve service was over and Franz had finished his "Merry Christmases" to everyone, he came back into the church to put his guitar away. He surprised Strauss, who was just then trying to sneak out of the instrument. It was too late. Franz had seen him.

"There you are, you little rascal," he said, laughing. "No need to be afraid. I won't hurt you."

Strauss stood as still as possible, wishing he could run. But his feet just wouldn't move.

Franz bent down slowly and spoke with a kind voice. "Oh, I wish I could make you understand," he said. "Sometimes I think God must look down from heaven at us a lot like I'm looking at you now. We humans don't really understand Him either. He's so big and powerful. I suppose that's why He gave us Christmas, to put His love in a size we can recognize and His forgiveness where we can reach it. I know you and your mouse friends didn't really mean to ruin the organ or upset the choir. I forgive you. Although..." he said, chuckling, "I think you enjoyed scaring poor Frau Hagglemeir."

Franz held out his hand and Strauss knew he could trust this gentle man. He climbed onto the hand and it lifted him out of the guitar and down to the floor. Strauss hesitated for a moment, looking intently into the big man's eyes as if to say "thank you". Then as quickly as his legs would move, he scurried through a hole and into the safety of the wall.

*J*ust inside, Strauss stopped and looked back. His heart was pounding, but not with fear. It was because Franz had been able to forgive them. The Mouse family would be able to live safely in St. Nicholas Church for many years to come. "Christmas is going to be extra special this year!" he said out loud to himself. Then he hurried over to join the other mice. He was just in time for the Mouse Christmas Eve party. No one noticed him at first, because everyone was talking at once.

"I thought for sure the Christmas Eve service was going to be ruined," said Herr Whiskers.

"I did too, after the crazy confusion Strauss caused," sighed Papa Mouse. "Why do humans get so upset? You'd have thought there was a cat in the room."

Auntie Wiggletail chimed in. "No fear of cats now! I just overheard Franz and Joseph talking. They agreed that no cats will be allowed in this church as long as they have anything to say about it." There was a general sigh of relief all around.

"And wasn't it a beautiful service!" said Mama Mouse.

Tiny Tot Mouse piped in, "Even Frau Hagglemeir liked it. Her face didn't look so much like pickle soup when she listened to the pretty Christmas song."

Everybody laughed. That's when they noticed that Strauss Mouse had joined them.

Mama Mouse shook her head and sighed, "Oh, Strauss, what will become of you?"

"I think I'll help Franz write some more songs," replied Strauss.

"NO!" everyone shouted in unison.

"Not that way!" he laughed. "But, maybe when the organ is fixed..."

"Maybe you should stick to the guitar," giggled Friedle. "That's where you seem to be most at home!"

The following spring, Karl Mauracher, the organ repairman, made his way to Oberndorf from Zillerthal. He had already heard about the organ-less Christmas Eve service and asked Franz for a copy of the carol everyone was talking about. Franz found one for him with just one thing missing—the writers' names. Before long, it was being performed by the Rainer family, a Tyrolean music group, and the Strasser family, glove makers who were also traveling folk singers. It became very popular all over the German-speaking countries of Europe, in Russia and eventually even across the ocean in America. For a long time, it was thought to be an anonymous folk song. Thirty-six years later, a government investigation discovered its true origin...or at least part of it.

Strauss has remained anonymous to this day. But now *you* know the important part he and his family played in the writing of this, one of the most beloved Christmas carols of all, *Silent Night*.